THE STORYBOOK
BASED ON THE MOVIE

THE STORYBOOK
BASED ON THE MOVIE

Storybook adaptation by Justine Korman

Based on the screenplay by
James V. Hart and Malia Scotch Marmo

From a screen story by
James V. Hart & Nick Castle

Photographs by Murray Close

Random House 🏠 New York

This book was prepared before the final editing of the motion picture,
and may contain some minor variations.

If you had been in London just before Christmas, you might have seen the Banning family step out of a taxi before No. 14 Kensington. They looked like an ordinary American family come for a holiday visit. They *were* a family, and they *had* come for a visit. But the things about to happen to them were far from ordinary!

The father, Peter Banning, changed everyone's watches from American time to British. He loved his pocket watch and always knew the precise time. He was a very busy, very important man, with Very Important Things to do, like Real Estate and Stocks and Bonds and Shares. He was always rushing somewhere in a car or in a plane, which he detested because he feared flying.

Peter carried a portable telephone on his hip. The phone was always ringing, and he was always talking about Very Important Business Deals whenever his son, Jack, or his daughter, Maggie, or even his lovely English wife, Moira, wanted his attention. Mr. Banning believed Business made the world go round, and he was, after all, providing for his family. So we must forgive Peter if he forgot Jack's baseball games or missed half of Maggie's school play.

Even by the time the Bannings got to London, Jack was still angry. Peter had missed his son's ball game. Maggie, however, didn't mind that he had been late for her play. She was still flying high from playing the part of her mother's famous Granny Wendy. You've heard of Wendy—the girl who went to Neverland with Peter Pan!

"Is Granny Wendy really the real Wendy?" Maggie asked.

Mr. Banning said, "No, not really," at the same time that Mrs. Banning said, "Yes, sort of." And Jack, who didn't care about Neverland, just tossed his favorite autographed baseball up and down, until his father made him put it away.

The door swung open before Mr. Banning could knock. And a sad old man peered out. Peter gasped, "Uncle Tootles?" The door slammed shut. Jack and Maggie giggled, and Mr. Banning told Jack to spit out his gum if he wanted to laugh.

The door popped open. A big bouncing dog gave them all a slobbery greeting. Liza, the maid, tried to restrain the huge Newfoundland—but it was like leashing the wind. "Nana!" chided Liza, who had been with Gran Wendy for many, many years. She welcomed the Bannings to the grand old home.

Elderly Uncle Tootles crawled on the floor, mumbling, "Lost my marbles. No more happy thoughts. Lost, lost, lost." The sad man smiled, then made a paper flower appear from nowhere and gave it to a delighted Maggie. Jack stepped back, afraid of his peculiar granduncle.

"I thought he was back in a home," Peter whispered.

But Gran Wendy would never have agreed to that. Tootles was her first orphan. Wendy was famous not only for her Neverland adventures but also for helping orphans. That's why an addition to a children's hospital was being named in her honor that very night at the Royal Hall.

Gran Wendy came down the stairs, ninety-two years old and lively as a spring day. She chirped at Peter, "Hello, boy!"

"Hello…Wendy." Mr. Banning apologized for being late. He'd been so busy with his Very Important Deal.…

"Never mind all that!" Gran Wendy smiled. "Come here and give me a squdge." She hugged each Banning in turn, then addressed the children. "There's one rule I insist be

obeyed in my house. No growing up. Stop this very instant!"
She looked at Peter. "That goes for you, too, Mr. Chairman-
of-the-Board Banning," she scolded. But Mr. Banning sighed
and said that it was too late.

Wendy wondered what was so Important about Mr. Banning's Terribly Important Business, and he explained about Ac-
quisitions and Mergers and Dabbling in Land Development.

Jack mocked, "Dad blows 'em out of the water."

"Peter, you've become a pirate!" Wendy exclaimed.

Snow gently fell on No. 14 while the grownups dressed
for the hospital dedication banquet. Mr. Banning had no time
to play with Maggie and Jack, who romped with Nana. Looking for a lost cuff link, Peter crawled around a chair and almost
bumped noses with Tootles, who was still searching for his
missing marbles.

Finally, Peter gave up and wandered into the nursery. The
cozy room was exactly as he remembered, except for something odd. Snow swirled beyond the window's lace curtains,
and when Peter looked down, he felt very dizzy.

He was glad when Moira called him to the phone on
Urgent Business. Peter's precious Deal was in danger. With
fearsome shouts he yelled and snapped at everyone to be quiet,
not caring at all about their feelings.

Wendy wistfully recalled when Peter was a young boy. They used to stand at the window and blow out the stars. How changed he was, this man who hadn't visited Granny for ten years and who never looked at his children except to scold.

Then Moira did some scolding of her own. "Peter, your kids love you. They want to play with you. How long do you think that lasts? Have fun with the children before they grow up!" Then to Peter's horror, Moira took the telephone and tossed the ringing thing out the window.

Down below in the snowy garden, Nana was taking out the garbage when she found the phone. After a quick sniff, she dug a hole and buried it.

"All children, except one, grow up," Gran Wendy read from an old copy of *Peter Pan and Wendy*. She was huddled with Maggie beneath a bedsheet tent in the nursery. Maggie was tying ribbons to the sheet to make a parachute for her father. Jack sulked on the ledge near the open French doors, pretending not to listen.

"When the first baby laughed for the first time, the laugh broke into a thousand pieces, and they all went skipping about—that was the beginning of faeries." Gran and Maggie laughed. "See where Jack is sitting?" Wendy asked. "That is the window Tink flew through, and this is the very room where we told stories about Peter and Neverland and old, scary Captain Hook!"

Mr. Banning came into the nursery, shuffling the notes for his dedication speech. Maggie gave her father the parachute as a hug, so he wouldn't be afraid of flying anymore. Suddenly, Peter dropped his notes and rushed to pull Jack away from the window. "Don't play near open windows!" he warned his son. "Don't we have windows at home?"

"Yeah, they have bars on them," Jack complained, searching for his baseball. "Hey, where's my ball?"

"The scary man at the window stoled it," Maggie replied.

"There is no scary man," Peter said. "I want that window locked for the rest of our visit." He asked Jack to be in charge while the grownups were gone. Then he gave his son the precious pocket watch and promised to be home soon. Jack winced. His father's promises always broke like cheap toys.

Maggie sniffed the flower Tootles had given her. "It smells nice!"

Peter put it in her hair and said, "It's paper, honey." Then he tucked her gently into bed, adding, "Slip into the envelope of your sheets and mail yourself off to sleep."

"Stamp me, mailman!" Maggie cooed. Peter kissed her twice for special delivery, and Moira sang a lullaby.

If stars could talk, they might have warned the Bannings hurrying to the Royal Hall. If snowflakes could whisper, the Bannings might have avoided the terrible trouble to come. But stars can only watch and wink, and snowflakes can only fall.

Peter Banning stumbled through his speech, wondering where his notes had gone. Finally he was forced to speak from his heart. "Wendy brought me in from the cold and taught me to read and write and found parents for me. I married her granddaughter. My kids love Wendy and want her to teach them to fly. If this wonderful woman has helped your life, stand up!"

The audience rose and cheered for Wendy. But the warm feeling chilled when the wind pushed into the Royal Hall and swirled its cruel cloak through the crowd. The ceremony was a success, but Gran Wendy felt tired and afraid.

The same wind twirled Peter's forgotten notes in the nursery. It was a breeze straight from Neverland, and it blew a gust of danger over the sleeping children. The night-lights yawned and nodded out. Nana barked unheeded in the garden, tugging at her chain leash.

When the Bannings returned to No. 14, they found the front door wide open, a deep scar gouged in the wood. Wendy turned pale, and Peter rushed inside. The lights were out, so he lit a candle to follow the gouge upstairs. Liza lay crumpled beside Nana, who scratched at the nursery door with her broken chain jangling. A crooked dagger pinned a parchment to the door:

Peter shrieked for his children amid the wreckage of the dark, empty nursery. Tootles cackled in the corner, "Have to fly, fight, crow! Save Maggie. Save Jack. Hooky's back!"

When the police arrived, they promised to do their best. But Gran Wendy said they could do nothing. "You may not remember, but the tales are true!" she told Peter. "Once you and I had wonderful adventures and laughed and cried and flew. Now Hook has come for revenge. To save your children, you must remember who you are!"

Alone in the nursery, Peter looked out the French windows at the starry sky. His children were missing, his wife was in shock, beloved Gran Wendy was talking utter nonsense. The Deal was on fire and sinking. Stronger men than he would weep at such a mess, and so did he.

Through the tears, his eyes were dazzled by a bright light which zigzagged into the room, bouncing off walls and knocking down pictures. Frightened, Peter rolled up a magazine and tried to swat the brilliant bug, tripping over dolls in his haste.

You would know this light was a faerie. But poor Peter had forgotten about faeries, as all grownups do. The light landed on a desk and became a tiny girl. She walked through an ink pad and marched up Peter's chest, tracking tiny footprints on his neat white shirt. She hovered nose to nose and sniffed him.

"It *is* you! A big you!" the faerie cried in delight. Her lovely voice tinkled like golden bells. Peter could only stare and stammer, "Wh...what kind of bug are you?"

"I'm no bug, but a faerie, a pixie. And if less is more, there's no end to me, Peter Pan," the faerie said proudly.

"Peter Banning," he sternly corrected.

The faerie shook her head in a spray of glimmering dust. "No one else has that smell of someone who's ridden the back of the wind, of a hundred fun summers sleeping in trees, and of adventures with Indians and pirates. You used to call me Tink."

Peter feared he was having a nervous breakdown. He said he didn't believe in faeries, and Tink burst into tears. "Every time someone says that, a faerie falls down dead. Now follow me and all will be well." She pulled on the rug and Peter fell, knocking himself senseless. Tink wrapped him in Maggie's parachute and carried him off to the second star to the left and straight on till morning.

You probably go to Neverland all the time in your dreams. But it's very hard to find the magic shores when you're awake, and nearly impossible if you're a grownup. However, Peter was carried there by a genuine faerie, and were her wings ever tired by the time they reached Pirate Square!

Peter slept along the way and woke with a terrible start. He was lying on a ledge across from a giant stuffed crocodile. The crowded town below bustled with peglegged pirates and sinister seadogs. Peter heard ringing, but it wasn't his missing phone. He thought he was having the worst nightmare ever, and his head hurt.

The parachute ripped, and Peter tumbled down. He crawled from beneath the sheet. Tink begged him to hide, but Peter wanted to find a phone and a drink of water and aspirin. He stumbled into a soup kitchen, marveling, "What a great dream!"

And that made Tink cross. She pricked Peter's hand with her tiny silver dagger to prove he was awake and in Neverland. "If you want to save Jack and Maggie, you'll have to fight Captain Hook," Tink said. "He plans a war!"

"I'm not going to swordfight this Hook person," Peter declared. "We'll talk this out like adults. Then I'll get my kids and go home. They can't miss any more school."

Peter should have known better than to walk into a pirate den unarmed. But he was just a grownup, and a rather silly one at that. Peter was shocked when the pirates tried to steal his fine clothes. If it wasn't for Tinkerbell, who knows what would have happened? As it was, the plucky pixie soon had the pirates wearing soup kettles and bruises.

No one but a pirate can cross Pirate Square, so Tink disguised Peter and hid in his hat. Peter heard a sea chantey and the whir of grinding metal as a blacksmith sharpened a shiny hook and placed it on a satin pillow. A fat little man grinned. "Sharp as a shark's tooth. Me Captain will be pleased."

Tink recognized the chubby fellow as Hook's henchman, Bosun Smee. "Follow that hook!" she whispered to Peter.

Soon they reached the pier where Hook's men tormented captive Lost Boys. "Hook's a scummy slaver," Tink explained. "He makes them count his treasure forever."

At the end of the pier, Hook's ship, the *Jolly Roger*, rode at anchor. She was a rakish craft, foul to the hull, with a massive

dark stern like a huge skull. Peter and Tink mingled with the scurvy scugs crowding the dirty decks. Tink recognized peculiar Noodler, and tattooed Bill Jukes, Skylights, Tickles, Gutless, Mullens, and other fierce faces.

Tickles played a fanfare on a concertina, and Long Tom, the cannon, boomed. Draped in velvet, jewels, and lace, Captain James Hook appeared on the deck, and his fearful crew clapped.

"What's with the hook?" Peter wondered.

"That handicap is your handiwork. You cut off his hand and threw it to the crocodile, remember?" Tink prompted.

"Of course. I've seen the video and Maggie's play."

"You slimy dogs said I was lazy and weak!" Hook thundered. "Who went to the other world? Who kidhooked Pan's brats?"

"Who killed and stuffed the cunning crocodile and made him into a quiet clock?" Smee echoed.

"Hook! Hook! Hook!" the pirates cheered.

Hook posed by a cloth dummy dressed as Peter Pan. "Ah, Pan! Fast, clever, cocky as a rooster, I'll grind your bones to dust and salt my food with you! I'll hurl you off the face of this cold earth forever!" Hook's sword sliced the dummy, and red sand rushed out and was swept away by the wind. "I shall have my glorious war, and I shall win!"

Hook called for the prisoners. A huge net rose from the hold, with Jack and Maggie huddled inside.

Peter could no longer hide. "Those are my kids! I'm their father!"

Tink cried, "Not now! You're not ready!"

Suddenly, Peter was surrounded by swords and daggers, and his courage failed. Hook stared. Was this fat fellow his great and worthy opponent? Hook swung his sword. "Stand back, scugs! He tricked Smee during the Tiger Lily incident, remember? Any moment Pan will pop out of that fleshy disguise. Prepare to die, Pan!"

"Uh, I can't fight you," Peter said reasonably.

Hook scowled. "Brimstone and gall! Who is this impostor? Smeeeeee! Check for the detail."

The bosun lifted Peter's shirt. "Arrr, there's the scar, Cap'n, the one you gave him when he rescued Tiger Lily."

"It cannot be!" Hook stared at Peter's sizable shadow darkening the deck. "This pasty codfish is not even a shadow of Peter Pan. Oh, what cruel hand has fate dealt me now?"

Peter had an idea. "Gentlemen, the stakes are high, but we can work this out. I want my children."

"And I want my war!" Hook growled. "Fight me with all the cleverness of the true Pan and win them back."

"Fight?" Peter produced his checkbook. "Let's get down to business, Hook. How much? I won't press charges."

"Bad form!" The pirate captain slammed Peter against
the mast, the hook at his nose.

"Mr. Hook, we could help each other," Peter babbled.
"This island is begging for condos. We could make millions!
You could be chairman of the board."

"I escaped death by crocodile, waited with nothing to do
but chase Lost Boys, and you are my reward?" Hook walked
away, disgusted. "Chairman of the board? You're worse than
me. I cannot soil my steel with your blood." Pirate swords
prodded Peter, forcing him down the plank.

"Hang on, Maggie! I'm here for you, Jack! I'll work it
out!" Peter promised, even as Jukes carried them off to join the
other slave children chained in the prison on the pier.

Hook smoked two cigars at once and brooded over his
lost war. Tink persuaded him to give her three days to get Peter

ready to fight. The captain cackled. "The ultimate battle — Hook vs. Pan! Children admitted free!" The crew cheered.

Then Hook ordered Peter to fly away.

"I can't!" he moaned.

Trying to totter back to the ship, Peter fell off the plank with a splash, sinking like a stone. Fearing all was lost, Tink flew away.

And indeed, Peter would have drowned if not for some beautiful mermaids who put him in a clamshell and pulled him up to the sandy shore.

You have, no doubt, seen the twin rainbows, the many moons and suns, the blue lagoon with flocks of flamingos and merry mermaids. But Peter had forgotten Neverland, and he scarcely believed his eyes. He took unsteady steps between sniffing, sneezing flowers until he tripped into a snare and swung upside down from a branch. Peter's struggles to free himself shook Tinkerbell from her tiny hanging house. Overjoyed to see Peter alive but wet, she snipped him free with golden scissors. Peter's first thought was to save his captive children.

"You'll need help!" Tink declared. She flew through the Nevertree, rousing Lost Boys, who leaped and swung from hut and hammock, down ladder and chute. Ace, No Nap, Too Small, Pockets, Thud Butt, and boys of every color and kind rushed to greet long lost Pan! But their excitement drained when they saw that Peter was old and fat. They wondered what their leader, Rufio, would say.

With a deafening crow, Rufio swooped down on a windcoaster, waving the shining sword of Pan.

"Okay, mister. Put that thing down before you poke someone's eye out!" Peter scolded. Then he demanded to talk to the grownup in charge.

"All grownups are pirates. We kill pirates," Rufio said.

"I'm not a pirate. I'm a lawyer," Peter corrected him.

"Kill the lawyer!" Rufio yelled. And the Lost Boys chased Peter around the Nevertree. Peter ran through a tunnel and along the windcoaster track. A group of Lost Boys followed, peppering him with stick-um arrows.

The arrows hit Peter in the chest.

"Glue? What is this?" Peter said, trying to remove the sticky stuff.

Almost immediately, Rufio and the rest were hot on his heels as Peter ran back to the Nevertree. He dodged snapping slingshots and swinging clubs. Rufio tapped Peter with the sword. "You're dead, jollymon! If you're the Pan, prove it! Can you fly? Can you fight? Can you crow?" Peter managed a feeble croak. Rufio sneered grandly.

"Silly boys! He can't do those things yet," Tinkerbell cried. "We have three days to get him ready to fight Hook."

Rufio refused to believe that Peter was Pan. The Boys agreed. Rufio had the Pan sword, so he was the leader. But then the Boys smoothed out Peter's wrinkles and looked deep into his eyes. "Oh, there you are!" Pockets said with a smile.

Rufio drew a line in the dirt, and the Lost Boys bounced back and forth over it, swayed by Rufio's doubts and Peter's pleas. They didn't know what to think, because they rarely thought at all!

"When Pan's away you always ask, what would Peter do?" Tink suggested. This set the Boys thinking. What *would* Peter do?

"I know!" Ace cried. "He'd get the Lost Boys back!"

"But aren't *you* the Lost Boys?" puzzled Peter asked. A jumble of voices told him many Boys had been snagged by Hook, who shot them from cannons and chained them to rocks and made the little ones crawl the plank. Even Rufio was afraid to rescue them without Pan.

"Survival of the fittest," Rufio said coldly. "Hook gets the slow ones. We're better off without them."

Peter swore he would do anything to get his kids back. Pockets thought Pan would talk like that, but Rufio's followers scoffed as the red sun sank in the Neversky.

Meanwhile, Captain Hook tossed away his dinner plate, too depressed to eat. A fat Pan had stolen his glorious war. "Hammer and tongs! Death's the only adventure left," Hook grumbled. He aimed a jeweled pistol at his head. Loyal as ever,

Smee wrestled Hook for the gun, toppling tables and tipping chairs. As Smee locked the pistol away, Hook complained, "Even this is no longer fun."

"There now, Cap'n. Things'll be bright in the morning," Smee said. "What kind of world would it be without Captain Hook? Aye? Let's get you in your cradle."

"Good form!" Hook hugged Smee, raking the bosun's back with his claw. Smee wriggled away from the painful embrace to help his captain undress for bed. Off came the tall boots and padded waistcoat, the great black wig, even Hook's bushy eyebrows, until all that was left of the dread pirate looked like a scrawny, balding boy.

"Sir! Lightnin' just struck me brains," Smee cried. "You could make Pan's children love you."

Hook shook his bare head. "No little children love me."

"You'd make a fine father, if I do say so," Smee said.

A red light glowed in Hook's evil eyes. "I do know a little about neglect," he admitted. "What a fine idea I've had! I shall not only destroy Pan, but I shall have his—*my*—children lead the battle! I shall be Captain Hook, family man!"

"'Tis the wickedest, prettiest policy ever I've heard," Smee praised. Hook fell asleep a happy villain.

The next morning, Hook played schoolmaster to students Jack and Maggie. The lesson was: WHY PARENTS HATE THEIR CHILDREN. Hook's plan was to convince the children that their parents had been happier before having children forced them to grow up.

Maggie cried, "They love us. You're a liar."

"I never lie!" Hook lied. "The truth is too much fun. What do your parents mean when they say, 'I love you'?"

Maggie raised her hand excitedly. "They mean we make them really, really happy all the time."

"Really, really wrong!" Hook shouted. A breathless

pirate burst into the room. "Captain, it's time to give the order for the firing squad." Hook excused himself, calmly stepped to the door, and gave the order to fire. The shots were still echoing when he turned to Maggie and said, "You flunk!"

Smee dragged Maggie out of the cabin. "This place makes you forget. Remember Mommy and Daddy love us!" she screamed.

Hook sneered. "Mommy and Daddy love you only when you do what they want: Wake up, get dressed, eat breakfast, say please, do your homework, stop acting like a child, and don't play near open windows! Ring a bell, Jack?" Then the ruthless captain reminded Jack of every time his father had let him down because of some Very Important Deal. He knelt beside the boy. "Did ye ever want to be a pirate, me hearty?"

"Just a baseball player," Jack breathed in awe.

"You can be anything you want on my team," Hook offered.

Across Neverland, Peter jogged through rain, snow, sunshine, and fallen leaves. Since Nevertime follows no schedule and changes as quickly as a Lost Boy's mind, Peter's training spanned all the seasons. His legs thought they had run at least two years. And his feet swore it was five. But his heart had the hardest time keeping hope alive despite the rude jeers of Rufio's gang.

Finally, Peter was ready to fly! Tink and the Boys tried everything they knew. Peter jumped off cliffs and branches and was finally strapped into a giant slingshot. Tink sprinkled him with pixie dust and told him to think happy! But serious adult thoughts canceled each idea. Cotton candy reminded him of cavities. Snow meant slush. And to grown-up Peter, spring and summer only meant taxes and mosquitoes.

"Doesn't anything make you happy?!" Tink was annoyed.

"Not being in this slingshot would make me very happy," Peter said just as Rufio slashed the rope. Peter hurtled through the air but swiftly sank into a safety net.

"I'm more man than Pan and twice the boy!" Rufio crowed. He left with most of the Lost Boys. Only Tink, Pockets, and a few others stayed to untangle muddy Peter.

Hungry, tired, and bandaged, Peter made his way back to the Nevertree. The Lost Boys were enjoying a banquet served on steaming platters, happily stuffing themselves with their favorite Neverfood: yams, mammee apples, and banana splash, washed down with calabashes of poepoe.

Peter eagerly lifted a lid, but he found the platter empty! "I don't get it! Where's the food?" he complained.

"Don't you have an imagination?" Tink asked. "Eat up."

"There's nothing to eat!" Peter spluttered.

"And plenty of it!" Tink replied, cheeks puffed with make-believe yams.

Rufio threw a tray at Peter's chest. Peter exploded. Enough was enough. "You're a badly raised child!" he shouted.

"You're a slug-eating worm," Rufio countered, and the

two engaged in a duel of insults with the Lost Boys keeping score. Once Peter got going, he topped them all and threw a fistful of imaginary food in Rufio's face. The food became real! Soon, Peter was licking yams off his own cheeks and laughing louder than he had in years. He was finally playing with the Boys.

Still angry, Rufio threw two coconuts straight at Peter's head. Ace shouted a warning, and someone tossed Peter a sword. Without thinking, Peter swirled and sliced. The coconuts fell in perfect halves! Everyone gasped, and Tink tugged on Rufio's earring. "Can't you see he's in there? Look in his eyes! Help him. Teach him to fight."

"Let go, you Neverbug!" Rufio scowled.

On the *Jolly Roger*'s deck, Jack, dressed like the captain, drilled a troop of scurvy seadogs. The men marched in faster and faster circles until Jack barked "Halt!" and they all crashed into one another. Evil pranced in Jack's eyes as he ordered, "Now kick the guy next to you!"

Maggie scolded her cackling brother through the prison bars. "Jack! Stop that! You think you're funny, but you wouldn't act this way if you weren't forgetting Mommy and Daddy."

Jack said he remembered them, and he ordered the pirates to salute the girl. "Girl?! I'm your sister!" Maggie screamed. "Don't forget Daddy and Mommy!"

One of the other children in the prison asked her what a Mommy was. Now, you and Maggie know that a mother is the cool side of a pillow when you flip it over, the sweet lips that kiss you good night, the calm, special someone who tidies your mind while you sleep so that when you wake up, all your nicest thoughts are right on top where you can find them. But since the captured kids had forgotten, Maggie explained. "A mommy is someone wonderful who feeds you and plays with you and takes care of you when you're sick and sings songs…"

"No, not songs, lullabies," a boy recalled dreamily.

So Maggie began to sing, and the sleepy children rested their heads on her lap. Jack almost remembered Moira's song, but Smee quickly distracted him. The captain lingered, listening in the shadows. Maggie was surprised, then realized, "That's why you're so sad. No one puts you to sleep. You need a mother!"

Hook's stern eyes softened, then he scoffed, "I'm sad because I have no war."

Far away on a branch of the Nevertree, Peter heard the familiar lullaby. Thud Butt joined him and said, "I remember Tootles. These are his happy thoughts. He lost them. They don't work for me. Maybe they'll work for you." He poured marbles like precious gems into Peter's hands. Peter hugged the little boy as two red suns sank into the Neversea.

When three suns rose over the *Jolly Roger* the next day, Hook snuggled in his bunk with his teddy bear, which had a hook for one of its paws. In Hook's dream of a lovely pirate war, cannons boomed and swords clashed and tick, tick, ticked like a hungry crocodile who had swallowed a clock.

The captain's mustache twitched to the rhythm, and he woke with his heart beating wildly. He followed the terrible ticking to Jack's hammock on deck. The captain's hook slowly slipped into the boy's pocket and gently removed Peter's pocket watch. Shaking with rage, Hook raised his iron claw. As his terrible shadow fell on the shivering boy, the ticking stopped.

Smee stood nearby, muffling the watch with his hands. "Cap'n, the little elf didn't know better."

Hook hesitated, then cried, "To the Ticktock Museum!"

With wicked glee, Hook displayed his vast collection of clocks and watches—all with faces smashed flat. "Each one tick-talked, and now listen!" the captain commanded eagerly.

"I don't hear anything," Jack said.

"Nothing left to tick," jolly Smee agreed.

"Good form! Exactly," Hook chortled. But just in case, he smashed a clock for the ticking that might have been, and another for dinner being late, and he invited Jack to join him. Soon Jack was smashing clocks for being told what to do all

day, and for brushing his teeth and combing his hair, and for having to make a little less noise. He and Hook had a glorious time smashing the clock museum. "For an ugly Pan!" Hook shrieked.

"Who wouldn't save us," Jack sobbed. "Daddy didn't even try." Hook put a gentle claw about the boy's shoulders.

"The question is, do you want to be saved?" Hook said. "Forget about home, the place of broken promises." He raised Jack's missing baseball. "Have I ever made a promise I haven't kept?"

Beneath the Nevertree, Peter pleaded with fierce Rufio to make his first fighting lesson easy. Tink stood on the end of Peter's sword and said, "Just do what you did with the coconut."

"That was a reflex," Peter stammered as the swords kissed. "I don't know how I did that."

Rufio counted, "Un, dos…" Just before "three," Rufio's blade slashed Peter's belt. Peter's pants fell to his ankles. The Lost Boys laughed. Rufio crowed. "Ya can't fly, ya can't fight, and mon, ya really can't crow!"

Pockets jumped up. "That's not fair. He hasn't done nothin' to make himself proud. How could he crow?"

This sparked a lively discussion. The Boys had many ideas. Peter could swallow fire, or write a letter, or stand on his head, or wrestle a bear... "Or he could go into town and steal Hook's hook!" Pockets cried. The Lost Boys cheered.

Before you could say "Hook is a crook," four peculiar pirates swaggered into town: Peter, and three sets of Lost Boys riding one another's shoulders in tottering towers. Through strangely empty streets the "pirates" headed for a hubbub in Pirate Square. They found a baseball field and seadogs playing catch in baseball uniforms.

Creeping under the bleachers, Peter spotted Jack taking his stance in the batter's box. From the stands, Hook called to Jack, "This makes up for all the games your Daddy missed. Hook would never miss your game." The pirate captain had captured Jack's heart as surely as if it were clamped in irons.

Hook tossed Jack's autographed ball to the umpire. A section of pirates held up cards that spelled out Jack's name as the boy stepped to the plate, swinging a peg-leg bat.

"Rip the bauble, Jack! Tear the leather off the orb!" Hook cheered. "Confound it, Smee! I need a glove!" The bosun replaced the hook with a glove, resting the cruel claw on the bleachers, inches from Peter's nose.

The Boys urged Peter to take the hook. Here was his chance to crow! But Peter could not take his eyes off Jack and Hook. Had his son forgotten him? Had he found another father?

Jack stared down at the pitcher as Smee loosed a whistling pitch. Jack braced himself at the plate. Peter tensed also. He knew Jack couldn't hit a curve ball.

Jack heard the pirates' roar and then the sharp *crack!* of the bat. His ball rocketed out of the park, soaring over Neverland.

Hook leaped to his feet, his eyes filled with real pride. "Did you see him? Oh, my Jack! You hit the curve ball!"

Peter was stunned. Jack capered around the bases, shaking every pirate's hand while Tickles played "For He's a Jolly Good Fellow." At home plate, Jack was hoisted onto Hook's shoulders. They paraded out of the park, followed by celebrating pirates.

Poor Peter! He had finally watched his son play baseball, and the victory was shared by his archenemy. Peter stood paralyzed with sadness. The hook lay forgotten on the bleachers. And the disgusted Lost Boys, who could never understand a father's loss, left him standing alone.

Peter wandered through Neverland in a daze, wracked with a terrible storm of emotion. He paced. He ran in circles around Round Pond. He hopped up and down, trying to fly. Then Jack's baseball streaked through the Neverleaves and struck his head.

Peter woke up groaning. His bleary eyes took in the rippling pond. When the waves stilled, a reflection smiled up at him—not the weary face of Peter Banning, corporate lawyer and failed father, but a wild-haired boy of fourteen, eyes full of mischief and adventure. He looked like Jack!

Peter heard the distant pirates chanting, "Jack, Jack, Jack!" He plucked Jack's prized ball from the pond. His chest swelled with a joy too great to contain. A victorious crowing leaped from his throat and echoed throughout Neverland.

Peter sprang atop a twisted root, poised to pounce on the next adventure. Someone's shadow rippled on the trunk of the great Nevertree. Peter turned to see who cast it, but the shadow grew from his own feet. Yet it had a life of its own!

The shadow showed him a huge face on the side of the tree. A knothole clogged with limbs and vines formed a crowing mouth. Peter tore away the debris until he could trace the crude letters carved in the bark: TOOTLES CURLY SLIGHTLY NIBS JOHN MICHAEL. Tears welled in his eyes for the days gone by. The knothole suddenly opened as if expecting him. Peter's shadow urged him to hurry. He squeezed in headfirst and tumbled into a murky cavern.

A tiny glow lit the darkness as dainty chimes rang. Tinkerbell twirled to show off her long, lovely gown. "What's the occasion?" Peter wondered, enchanted by her beauty.

"You are. It's a welcome home party!" Tink's glow brightened to reveal the Home Underground. Once upon a time, in this simple room rough as a cave carved by baby bears, Wendy had played mother to him and the Lost Boys. Peter recognized the burned stump of the Nevertree they had used as a table and the walk-in fireplace where Wendy had hung the wash. Nothing was left of the beds but blackened boards and ashes.

Tinkerbell stood in the niche that had been her private apartment. Cobwebs had replaced the tiny curtained door. The faerie said, "Hook burned the Home when you didn't come back."

Peter rummaged through the ruins. "This is Wendy's house. Tootles and Nibs built it for her. I remember." He gaped in amazement. "I remember! Wendy used to tell us stories while she darned our socks. Little Michael's basket bed was here, and John slept here."

He kicked the charred remains of his youth, and something caught his eye. "Taddy!" Peter tenderly lifted a burned teddy bear from the ashes and hugged it. "My mother put Taddy in my pram to keep me company."

"What else can you remember?" Tink prompted.

"When I was a baby, I lay in my pram watching birds swoop while my parents planned my future: the best schools, a good job, what a fine man I would be. But I didn't want to be a man. I wanted to always be a little boy and have fun. I thrashed and kicked until the pram rolled off to Kensington Gardens. There I lived among the birds and faeries for a long time till you sprinkled me with pixie dust and we flew away to Neverland. I came home once, but they had forgotten me."

Tink stretched her wings and sighed. Pan was back!

"I found other windows that weren't closed," Peter recalled. "That's how I met Wendy. I lost my shadow in her nursery. I came back for it but couldn't stick it on, even with soap. Then Wendy woke up and said, 'Boy, why are you crying?' I allowed her to stitch my shadow to my toes and brought her back to Neverland to be a mother to us all."

A flood of memories washed over Peter. What fun he'd had in Mermaid Lagoon, tossing rainbow bubbles. And what about the time he rescued Tiger Lily and was slashed by Captain Hook's claw? The old villain left him and Wendy on Marooner's Rock to drown in the rising tide. But Wendy flew away on Michael's kite, and the Neverbird saved Peter with her floating nest. Then there was the Night of Nights, when Hook's scugs kidnapped Wendy and the Lost Boys. Peter crowed. How cleverly he rescued them!

Tink glowered. "I'm glad Wendy couldn't stay. She was a great ugly girl, the silly thing!"

Peter laughed. "You were jealous! When she kissed me, you pulled her hair. Wendy called a thimble a kiss and a kiss a thimble. It took me years to figure out which was which.

"Many times I brought her back to Neverland for spring cleaning, and each time she was older. She finally forgot how to fly! The last time I went to see her, she had a granddaughter." Peter's voice choked remembering his first sight of Moira. "She was so lovely I wanted to give her a real kiss, not a thimble, and I stayed. Wendy found me parents. Then there was school, and I grew up."

Tink sniffled, remembering how she had been locked outside Wendy's window years ago. Poor Tink could not stop Pan from giving up Neverland. "I see why you have trouble finding a happy thought. So many sad memories."

Peter flung Taddy in the air as if to rid himself of the painful past. He missed Moira and the children. Now he regretted all the times he'd stayed at the office when he should have been home. Peter never meant to neglect his family, he just got caught up in grown-up games, as children sometimes will when playing pretend. And no one had tidied his mind for the longest time, so it was cluttered with stock prices and the details of deals.

The charred bear twirled in the air, and Peter wanted to hug the scorched toy once more. When he did, Taddy seemed to be a happy four-year-old Jack, and Peter dimly heard baby Maggie's angel voice calling, "Fly me, Daddy!" He twirled the children around. They laughed and pulled his hair and tugged his nose. Moira twirled with them. And Peter realized he loved his family and was lucky to be a part of them. "Tink! I did it! I did it! I found my happy thought—" Bouncing like a mad moonbeam, Peter Pan crowed, "I can fly!"

"Follow me, and all will be well!" Tink shouted, spiraling through the heart of the Nevertree's trunk. Pixie dust sprayed in Peter Pan's face as they shot from a hollow limb up through the canopy of Neverleaves. Pan did a perfect jackknife dive, buzzing like an airplane, swooping through the clouds.

All children are birds before they are babies. If you remember being a bird, you know how Peter Pan felt riding the back of the wind. He laughed in the sky, as he had when he snatched food from the eagles to feed Wendy on her journey to Neverland years before.

Pan whooshed like a meteor to swoop over the Lost Boys' war council crouched in the roots of the Nevertree. The Boys turned their faces skyward. Jaws dropped in awe. Pockets fell flat on his back and shrieked with joy. "It's really Pan!"

Only Rufio remained intent on the plans to attack the *Jolly Roger* that were drawn in the dirt. That is why he did not see Pan flying swift as a swallow behind him. He only felt sudden cold, for Peter Pan snatched Rufio's belt, and the boy's pants dropped to his ankles. Pan crowed above his rival, then skimmed the Round Pond and squirted water in Rufio's astonished face. The Lost Boys tumbled and rolled, sides aching with laughter.

Pan basked in admiration. He hugged Pockets as Lost Boys jumped and leaped all around them. Raging, Rufio ran to his treehut, and his war whoop split the air. He swung the Pan sword in gleaming circles. Frightened Boys scampered to safety behind their new captain. Ace cried a warning.

But instead of striking, Rufio knelt and offered the hilt of the sword to Peter Pan. "You can fly, you can fight, you can crow," Rufio said reverently. Behind him, three sinking suns painted the Neversea red.

The Lost Boys reveled around blazing bonfires. Peter Pan missed Tink and rose through swirling sparks to her tiny house. Pan's shadow danced in the moonlight while Tink talked about old times. Tink had always loved Pan and had even drunk poison to save his life. Now the faerie feared she would lose Pan again because she was too small. So she made the only wish she had ever wanted for herself. The faerie grew and grew until she was as large as her love. Tink's tiny house perched on her head like a hat, her glow bright as day. Peter Pan's shadow fled in alarm.

Pan was speechless as Tink murmured, "I'm going to give you a kiss." Peter Pan put out his hand, expecting a thimble. But Tink really kissed him! The kiss reminded him of Moira and his children, and his eyes drifted to the pirate ship in the harbor.

"What are you looking at?" Tink asked, knowing the answer. "Go save your kids, you silly man!"

Dawn's rays gleamed on musket and sword as Hook beamed with pride aboard the *Jolly Roger* and harangued the assembled crew. "Split my infinitives! 'Tis my hour of triumph! Today's war won and Pan's bones charred to dust, I shall leave this shadow world and take my rightful place in history."

The concertina fell silent at the sound of ripping canvas. "Cap'n! It's a ghost! The ship's haunted. We're doomed!" Smee cried. He stared at a shadow spotlighted by the sun.

"What's that?" Jack asked.

Pan parted a slashed sail and slid down a sunbeam, shouting, "Peter Pan the Avenger!"

Smee cowered behind his fearless captain while Hook gloated. "Do my eyes deceive me? Peter Pan! Has it been three days? Time flies and so do you! Good form! How did you manage to fit into those smashing tights again?" The pirates laughed with evil glee.

Blushing, Pan glanced down at his legs. "Hand over my children now, codfish, and you and your men go free," he said firmly.

Hook was never more sinister than when he was polite. He graciously suggested that Pan ask Jack what he wanted.

"Take my hand, Jack, we're going home," Peter Pan said.

"I am home," the miniature pirate replied, and Hook put a fatherly arm around the boy's shoulder.

"Good form! You see? He is my loving son, and I am prepared to fight for him," Hook exclaimed, and drew his sword. "Peter Pan, prepare to meet thy doom!"

"Dark and sinister man, have at thee!" cried Peter Pan.

Tickles pumped a happy tune, and the scugs rushed to the fray, led by Noodler and Jukes. Peter Pan faced the scurvy crew with his sword and dagger flashing. The morning air rang with clashing steel and fearsome shouts.

"Don't you love being a pirate, Jack?" Hook yelled as Peter Pan bravely battled a score of greasy seadogs.

Deep inside Jack, among the old hopes and old hurts, a glimmer of recognition stirred. He asked, "Don't I know him?"

"You've never seen him before in your life," Hook lied.

Pan flew straight up to the yardarm and crowed in the rigging. "I found my happy thought, Jack. It was you!"

The captain's hook chopped at a thick rope.

"Dad! Look out!" Jack called, but too late!

The rope whipped free and a heavy net fell, dragging Peter Pan down to the dirty deck. Pan cried, "Bangerang!" And the Lost Boys echoed, "Bangerang!" With Rufio in the lead, they swung and catapulted, raining like howling hail onto the *Jolly Roger*. Hook cried to Smee, "Call out the Village Militia!"

Even as Smee hurried to sound the alarm, Lost Boys swarmed the ship's rigging and the battle was joined.

Rufio fought his way over toward Peter, and back-to-back the two friends fended off the pirates.

Screams and war cries cut the air, thick with clashing swords and crashing clubs. "Jack, watch this!" Pan cried. "We'll show you who's chicken!"

Ace aimed a fast-firing eggshooter, coating the pirates in gloppy goo. The Lost Boys blasted with blowguns and sling-shots, tomato catapults and marble guns. Pan and his band guffawed as pirates slipped and slid and flipped and fell on the sloppy deck. Hook despaired while cowardly Smee hid below.

Thud Butt crouched on the slippery planks and curled into a ball. The rumbling Thudball rolled like a bowling ball,

toppling pirates right and left. But when he stood, Thud Butt was captured. "Help!" he shrieked. Jack grabbed a rope and swooped to the rescue. He freed the grateful Thud Butt, but was himself seized by Noodler. Just then, the Village Militia arrived to reinforce the desperate pirates. In the confusion, Rufio saw a chance to make his move against Captain Hook.

Meanwhile, in the gloomy prison, Maggie and the slave boys plotted their escape. One boy threw a rope made of torn tapestries out the window. But just then, the jailer came into the room. "Get away from that window! There's a war on!"

The jailer charged Maggie, who cried, "Jack! Help!"

Outside, Rufio and Hook crossed swords, but Pan intervened. "Hook's mine," he said. Then he heard Maggie and hurried to help.

Maggie was bewildered when Peter Pan landed in the jail. "Daddy? My daddy is Peter Pan?" she gasped as Pan and the jailer exchanged blows. Pan tipped a statue atop the jailer, and the pinned wretch pleaded, "Get it off me!"

"I'll never lose you again," Peter promised his daughter.

"Stamp me, mailman." Maggie smiled. And in front of the stunned Lost Boys, Peter kissed her forehead.

"Guard her while I get Jack," Pan commanded, and flew off.

Latchboy gaped at Maggie. "Are you a girl?"

Jack had never seen anything like the battle raging on the decks of the *Jolly Roger*. He watched as Hook and Rufio circled each other with whistling steel and agile steps. With a flurry of blows, Hook drove Rufio backward, but his blade struck the clanging bell. Now Rufio took the offensive, and Hook minced away. But the sly captain's skillful claw slipped the sword from Rufio's grip. The Lost Boy dived to the deck to seize his weapon. As the wicked captain approached, Rufio jeered, "Looky, looky. I got Hooky."

"Sadly, you have no future as a poet," Hook said. His eyes gleamed red as he ran his cold blade through Rufio. Just as the boy fell, Peter Pan swooped down to cradle Rufio's head.

"You know what I wish?" Rufio whispered. "I wish I had a dad like you." Those were the last words on his last breath.

"Bad form! He's only a boy like me," Jack murmured. "Dad, take me home."

"You *are* home," Captain Hook asserted. But Jack flung his pirate hat at the wicked man's face.

Peter Pan swept Jack up in his arms and flew to the wharf.

"Peter Pan, I'll always be your worst nightmare come true. Come back and fight me now, or I'll be back! You can't escape me!" But there was no answer to Hook's hoarse shout,

only the sounds of scattered fighting as his crew was over-whelmed by the Lost Boys.

Big, strong, and ruthless, the pirates would have whipped the prankish boys if they had fought together. But the seadogs struck wildly, every scug for himself. Many abandoned ship with the Lost Boys at their cowardly heels. Hook heard the distant din of battle in the town. He knew all was lost, but Hook would never surrender, so he pursued his enemy.

Brilliant blades ringing, Hook and Pan dueled down the gangplank into Pirate Square.

"Rippingly good comeback!" Hook cheered. "Three days! Diet? Exercise? A miracle must have restored a fat old Pan!"

If you had been in Pirate Square, you would have seen the most amazing sight. Peter Pan swooped and soared, circling the slashing sword of Captain Hook. The two foes fought in the streets and in the shops, upstairs and down, over chairs and under laundry, hacking and cutting as if they'd never tire.

"Bad form! Play fair," Hook complained. "Stop hovering. I can't reach you up there."

"And you with only one hand," Pan teased. But nevertheless he alighted to fight on dancing feet.

The captain bowed courteously. "Thank you."

With a treacherous move, Hook forced Peter's face close to a spinning grindstone outside the Pirate Mill. The captain sneered, "Alas! This is all a dream. When you wake, you won't be Peter Pan, but old Peter Banning, a cold, selfish man who is obsessed with success and hides from his family."

Jack pushed through the crowd toward his discouraged father. "You *are* the Pan!" he said with faith and love.

Pockets echoed the phrase, and the Lost Boys took up the chant. Peter Pan believed in himself again, and in the blink of an eye, Hook was disarmed. Pan gallantly returned Hook's sword.

"Curse you for your eternal good form!" the captain cried. And the fighting began anew. "Who and what art thou, Pan?"

"I am youth. I am joy. I will fight you, James Hook!"

Suddenly, Pirate Square was filled with Lost Boys carrying clocks. The wretched captain faced the steadily marching hands of hundreds of tick-tick-ticking timepieces everywhere he turned. Hook recoiled from the hated sound, curling like a burned match. Yet the captain was prepared to fight to the last, even though his enemy nimbly sidestepped every thrust and jab.

Peter Pan taunted, "Ticktock, ticktock, Hook's afraid of the old dead croc. I think not. I think James Hook is afraid of time ticking away." Twisting his wrist, Pan disarmed Hook.

The old captain fell to his knees, breathless and exhausted. "Good form, Peter. I am fallen."

Pan pressed the point of his blade at Hook's throat. "You killed Rufio. You kidnapped my children. You deserve to die!"

Hook lifted his chin smugly in a heroic pose. "Strike true, Peter Pan!"

The square was silent. Would Pan kill Captain Hook? Maggie tugged Pan's trembling arm. "Let's go home. Please,

Daddy? He's just a mixed-up sad old man who needs a mommy."

"Yeah," Jack agreed. "Let's go. He can't hurt us."

Tears welled in Hook's forget-me-not eyes. "Bless you, child," the captain quavered. "Good form, Jack!"

Pan reluctantly sheathed his sword. "Take your ship and never come back to Neverland again." Hook groveled as the crowd cheered, and Peter led his children away. Suddenly, a slender knife sprang into Hook's hand. That treacherous fiend had more than lace up his sleeve! "Fools! James Hook *is* Neverland!"

"Peter! Look out!" Too Small shouted. But before Pan could draw his sword, Hook had pinned him against the scaly belly of the stuffed crocodile.

"You broke your promise," Pan protested.

"I've waited long to shake your hand with this!" Hook snarled, raising his cruel claw. "From evermore, when children read of you, it will say, 'Thus perished Peter Pan.'"

Unseen by anyone, Tinkerbell was nearby. She watched

the captain threaten Peter with his hook. And just as the shining point slashed, a flash of light struck like a tiny lightning bolt. Brave Tinkerbell deflected the captain's blow, and his hook plunged into the croc's belly.

Hook's struggle to free his claw toppled the tower. As the crowd fled, Pan pulled Jack and Maggie to safety. The crashing croc swallowed Hook in its great grinning jaws.

As the dust settled in the square, the Lost Boys and Peter and all looked upon the fallen croc in wonderment. Too Small crept close and peeked within the yellow fangs. "Hook's gone!"

"Bangerang!" Pan crowed. "Bangerang!" the Lost Boys cheered, capering in a victory parade around Pirate Square.

"Hurray for Pan the Man!" Peter applauded himself. Then he saw Jack, Maggie, and Tink waiting for him. He could not stay and play. He had done what he had come to do; time to go home.

Tink sprinkled the children with faerie dust. "One happy thought is all you need."

"Mommy!" Maggie beamed and floated upward.

"My dad is Peter Pan," Jack said, joyfully rising.

But before he left, Pan chose a new leader for the Lost Boys. "I'll never forget you this time," he promised. "You're all my boys." Then he entrusted the Pan sword to Thud Butt. "Take care of everyone smaller than you," Peter said.

Thud Butt raised the sword. "Peter Pan forever!"

From a dinghy laden with treasure and a pretty mermaid, Mr. Smee saw the family Pan fly higher and higher until they were lost among the fluffy clouds. Smee sighed. "Poor Cap'n, he hates happy endings."

The first rays of dawn chased the shadows of Neverland from the nursery at No. 14 Kensington. Night-lights burned above Moira, who slept in a rocking chair. A Neverland breeze blew open the window, and Jack landed on the balcony, with Maggie riding piggyback. "Who is that lady?" Jack asked.

Maggie rubbed sleep from her eyes. "It's Mother!" And when she said it, Jack remembered. "She looks like an angel," Maggie said. "Let's not wake her yet."

So the two tired children climbed into their warm beds to hide under the covers. Moira stirred and saw the open window. She rose and locked it tight. When she saw the lumps in the beds, she did not believe her eyes, because she had seen them so often in her dreams. Gran Wendy joined her in the nursery.

Gran gasped as Jack popped up. "Mom!" was all he could say before he began to cry. Maggie popped into her mother's arms with a happy squeak. "Mommy!"

"Oh, my babies!" Moira wrapped her arms around her children, smothering Jack and Maggie with kisses and tears.

Jack said, "There were all these pirates! I almost…"

"Daddy saved us!" Maggie interrupted. "We flew!" and the little girl gave Gran Wendy a big squdge.

Gran cooed, "Pirates? You flew? How lovely!"

Peter woke to the sound of a groundskeeper sweeping up empty bottles. He sat up in Kensington Gardens. Tink stood on the bronze shoulder of a statue of Peter Pan. "You know that place between sleep and dreaming? That's where I'll always love you, Peter Pan. And that's where I'll wait for you to come back."

And then the rising sun blinded him. When Peter looked again, Tinkerbell was gone with his memory of Neverland. But he was changed. Peter danced and sang and laughed his way back to No. 14, not caring what anyone thought. He vaulted the terrace wall and did a triple flip into the garden.

He heard a muffled ringing and dug up the phone Nana had buried. "Brad, hi! I'm sitting in the snow. How am I? I'm greater than good and much gooder than great."

Peter climbed the drainpipe to the nursery window, pounding on the glass until the window swung wide.

"What have I told you about this window?" Peter demanded of Jack. "Keep it open! Don't ever close it!" Peter hugged his son and flew him around the room. Then it was

Maggie's turn, and Moira's, until they were giddy with laughter.

Peter took the pouch of marbles from around his neck and poured happy thoughts into old Tootles's gnarled hands. "Look! I didn't lose my marbles after all," Tootles said. He wandered to the window, lost in memories.

Wendy took Peter's hand. "Hello, boy."

"Hello, Wendy."

"Boy, why are you crying?" Wendy asked, as she had long ago.

"I don't know. It's just a tear for every happy thought."

Tootles sprinkled faerie dust on himself from the pouch and began to rise. Peter and his family were amazed—they couldn't believe their eyes.

"Thank you—good-bye!" Tootles said. He turned and flew out the window. "Seize the day!" he called back to them.

Wendy looked at Peter. "So your adventures are over," she said.

Peter sighed. "Oh, no...to live—to live will be an awfully big adventure."